Translated from the French by Claudia Zoe Bedrick

www.enchantedlion.com

Book Design: Jonathan Yamakami

First published in 2016 by Enchanted Lion Books,
351 Van Brunt Street, Brooklyn, NY 11231

A CIP record is on file with the Library of Congress

ISBN 978-1-59270-196-4

Printed in China by RR Donnelley Asia Printing Solutions Ltd.

1 3 5 7 9 10 8 6 4 2

Words and Pictures by Kerascoët

ENCHANTED LION BOOKS
NEW YORK

Paul and his sister Antoinette are having breakfast. The smell of warm rolls hovers in the air.

Antoinette piles jam and chocolate on her special Two-Taste Toasts. She loves making these so much that if the honey pot weren't empty, she would make Three-Taste Toasts!

"Want one, Paul?" she asks, opening her mouth for another bite.

"No thanks," says Paul politely, enjoying his toast spread neatly with butter.

Every morning, Paul and Antoinette divide the chores.

Antoinette loves clearing the table. Licking the plates and sticky knives is her favorite thing!

Paul prefers tidying up, making sure everything is sparkling and in its place.

After clean up, Antoinette wants to go outside.
"Come on, Paul! Let's go hunting for earthworms!"

Paul mumbles something through his toothbrush.
But Antoinette isn't listening anyway.

"Maybe we'll find a dead bird," Antoinette continues, "or lots of big shiny-backed beetles. The first one to catch a lizard wins!"

"Antoinette, there's just a short something I need to do first. Then we'll see."

Antoinette follows as Paul goes to do his “short something.”

Antoinette soon realizes that Paul has a very different plan for his day in mind.

After what seems like forever,
Paul finally stands up.
Antoinette doesn’t waste a second.

“Come on, Paul! Now’s our chance or we’ll never leave this gloomy house!” Antoinette knows that Paul doesn’t like going outside very much at all.

But once he does, Paul can't help looking around
for something interesting to do.

When Paul sees beautiful gold button flowers in the meadow, he's inspired to think deeply about Ikebana, the Japanese art of flower arranging. He's been reading about it every night before he falls asleep.

Antoinette prefers playing with wild animals.

“This snail is soooo delicious!” she says gleefully.
“Don’t you want just a tiny taste of Edmond?”

Paul feels queasy just looking at Edmond.

Antoinette slips the poor little snail into her pocket for later.

Then she's off, throwing herself upon the back of a ferocious beast. Paul sees danger.

Is it a bison? A yeti? A werewolf?

For Antoinette, it's love at first sight.

"If we keep him," she sighs, "we can teach him to do tricks."

Paul is completely put out, but Antoinette remains unruffled by his bad humor.

"Oh calm down, Paul, and taste these blackberries. They're sooooo sweet!" Antoinette shovels berries into her mouth, the dog already forgotten.

"You're going to get into trouble with the berry fairy if you eat them that way," Paul replies coolly.

"Really?" asks Antoinette, her cheeks stuffed with berries. "Why?"

But before Paul can answer,
Antoinette already has a new idea.

Gathering up a spider's web, she bunches it up, making it look like a giant cotton candy. (If cotton candy was full of bugs and spiders!)

"Now it's a beautiful beard," she exclaims. "You look so handsome, Paul."

"I'm touched," Paul says, shuddering as a spider crawls onto his arm. "But please take it off right now. It's very fragile and will get destroyed."

"Nobody really likes spiders you know," Paul says. "Flowers are a much better way of saying thank you. Each one also means something. The gold button evokes joy, the daisy embodies innocence, the red poppy signifies remembrance. But watch out for digitalis—it's poisonous!"

Antoinette listens impatiently to Paul's endless explanations.

Finally, when she can't take it anymore, she breaks into a run.

"Watch out for puddles!" Paul warns her, hanging back cautiously.

But Antoinette's delight is so infectious that Paul joins in, leaping elegantly over each puddle.

Antoinette doesn't miss a single one!

Now that Antoinette is covered in mud, it's time to return home.

Breathless from running, Antoinette asks, “ Paul, are you angry with me?”

“No, of course not,” Paul says flatly. “It’s just time for me to clean up. You can do whatever you like.”

Antoinette knows there's no point in talking to Paul until everything is clean as a whistle.

As Paul cleans, he plays his favorite game.

A while later, when she's sure Paul is tucked into crisp pajamas, Antoinette comes to find him.

"Are you all done, Paul?"

"Oh, yes," Paul says, slightly startled. "I've just been thinking a little."

"Well, now you have to come with me," Antoinette says brightly. "I have a surprise for you!"

Antoinette leads Paul into the kitchen. She has made him her famous Everything Tart!

After polishing off the tart, Paul and Antoinette snuggle up, surrounded by the scents of the day. Soon it will be bedtime. After such a busy day, they are sure to sleep well.

But where their dreams might take them, well, that's a whole other story.

The End